AR 3.0
pts 0.5
z 167815

Army Rangers

BY LINDA BOZZO

Amicus High Interest is an imprint of Amicus
P.O. Box 1329, Mankato, MN 56002
www.amicuspublishing.us

Copyright © 2015 Amicus. International copyright reserved in all countries. No part of this book may be reproduced in any form without written permission from the publisher.

Library of Congress Cataloging-in-Publication Data
Bozzo, Linda.
Army Rangers / by Linda Bozzo.
 pages cm. – (Serving in the military)
Includes index.
Summary: "An introduction to the life of Army Rangers in the US Army Special Operations Command (USASOC) describing some missions, how they train, and their role in the armed forces"– Provided by publisher.
ISBN 978-1-60753-490-7 (library bound)
ISBN 978-1-60753-633-8 (ebook)
1. United States. Army. Ranger Regiment, 75th–Juvenile literature. 2. United States. Army–Commando troops–Juvenile literature. I. Title.
UA34.R36B69 2015
356'.1670973–dc23
                         2013039228

Editor: Wendy Dieker
Series Designer: Kathleen Petelinsek
Book Designer: Steve Christensen
Photo Researcher: Kurtis Kinneman

Photo Credits: Stocktrek Images/Superstock, cover; Stocktrek Images, Inc./Alamy, 5; US Army Photo/Alamy, 6; Corbis, 8/9; Robert Benson/Aurora Photos/Corbis, 10; .S. Department of Defense/Science Faction/SuperStock, 12/13; David Howells/Corbis, 14; Rob Howard/Corbis, 17; Trinity Mirror/Mirrorpix/Alamy, 18; Terry Moore/Stocktrek Images/Corbis, 21; LEE JAE-WON/Reuters/Corbis, 22/23; DOD Photo/Alamy, 25; StockTrek Images/SuperStock, 26; byllwill/Getty, 29

Printed in the United States at Corporate Graphics in North Mankato, Minnesota.

10 9 8 7 6 5 4 3 2 1

Table of Contents

A Ranger Night Raid	4
Ranger School	11
The Home Front	19
Overseas	23
Serving Our Country	28
Glossary	30
Read More	31
Websites	31
Index	32

A Ranger Night Raid

The year is 2012. A team of U.S. Army Rangers leads a **raid** in Afghanistan. They are looking for enemy soldiers. In the dark of night, they search **compounds**. Some go into a building. Others are on the roof. Gunfire breaks out! Two Rangers on the roof are shot.

How can Army Rangers see during night missions?

The pilot looks for enemy soldiers.

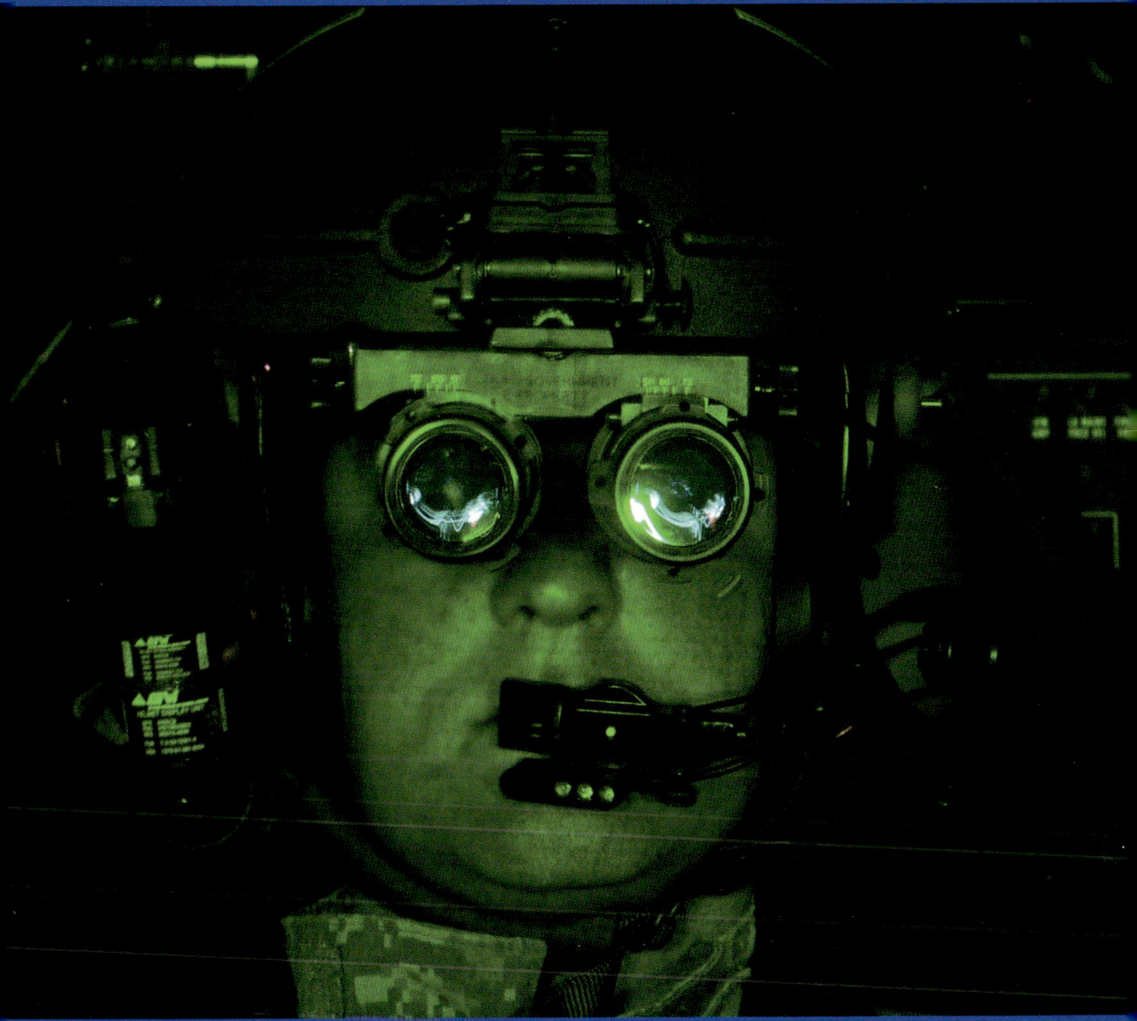

 Rangers wear NVGs, or Night Vision Goggles. These goggles help them see in the dark.

Soldiers drop down from a helicopter.

The Rangers fire back. One Ranger races up a ladder. He finds the hurt soldiers. The enemy keeps firing! More gunshots ring out. The Ranger shoots back. He has to do something to save his hurt teammates.

Then the Ranger throws two **grenades** into the building. Boom! They explode. The blast gives his team more time. They move the two hurt Rangers to safety. Rangers keep shooting. Enemy soldiers are shot and killed. The building is cleared. Mission accomplished!

Rangers are ready to go in the door.

Soldiers lift logs to train.
It helps them build strength.

Q Do you have to start in the U.S. Army to become a Ranger?

Ranger School

Army Rangers are a special unit of the U.S. Army. Rangers train to go farther and move faster. They train to fight harder. They learn to fight with and without **weapons**. Rangers often lead special missions. They lead teams in war. The first step to becoming a Ranger is to go to Ranger School.

 No. Most Rangers start as army soldiers. But some come from the U.S. Navy, U.S. Air Force, or U.S. Marines.

Soldiers **volunteer** to go to Ranger School. They are trained in three stages. The first step is "crawl." When they pass, they go onto the "walk" stage. The soldiers who pass that stage go onto the "run" stage. Each step is very hard. Many soldiers do not pass. They do not become Rangers.

Rangers even train in mud!

A soldier uses a tool to check the weather. He needs to be ready.

During the three stages, Rangers train to work in all kinds of places. They learn to climb down steep cliffs with ropes. They learn to stay dry in the jungle. They learn to find water in the desert. Day and night, Rangers train. Eat? Sleep? There is not much time for that.

Rangers learn many skills at Ranger School. They learn how to use all kinds of weapons. They learn survival skills. Rangers train to fight in small teams. They learn to strike quickly. They are known for surprising the enemy. They must complete their missions before the enemy knows what is happening.

Why do Army Rangers train to fight in small groups?

The soldiers learn to use tools to spot things far away.

 Large groups of soldiers can be easily seen. Small groups can move more quickly.

Rangers arrive home after a mission.

The Home Front

On the home front, Rangers spend most of their days training. They plan and prepare for real missions. This means practicing drills as if they are real missions. Every Ranger must know his job. Some get gear ready. Others make sure weapons work or pack supplies.

At home in the United States, teams of Rangers wait for a call. They are ready to go to war on short notice. Rangers move quickly anywhere in the world. When they complete their mission, they return home. The home front is where Rangers rest.

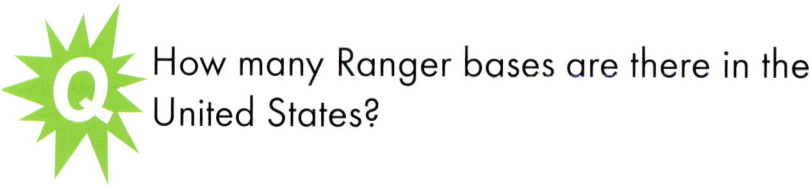

How many Ranger bases are there in the United States?

Helicopters bring Rangers to combat.

 Four. Three are in Georgia and one is in the state of Washington.

Overseas

Army Rangers are sent all over the world. Rangers sneak deep into enemy territory. They arrive by land, sea, or air. They drop from choppers using ropes. They **parachute** from planes. Rangers will cross rivers and swamps to get to the trouble. They are ready for anything.

Rangers ride in a truck. They are always ready to go.

Rangers go to the fight. They see **combat** often. Attacks are quick. Rangers might take over enemy airfields. They might raid buildings where the enemy hides. They might bomb buildings where enemy supplies are kept. The mission could take days. It could take weeks. But they will get the job done.

 Why do Rangers take over enemy airfields?

Rangers move quickly on missions.

 Rangers take over so U.S. troops can use them. Other soldiers bring in supplies or send attack planes.

The Rangers hide to spy on the enemy.

Rangers are good spies. They watch the enemy. They learn where people are. They make maps of buildings. They help plan attacks.

Rangers might rescue soldiers who are in trouble. They get soldiers out of enemy prisons. They help people who are hurt. Army Rangers get the job done!

Serving Our Country

The Army Ranger motto is "Rangers Lead the Way." Rangers lead the way into war. Rangers are the first to the fight. The enemy can attack anywhere, at anytime. Rangers move farther and faster. They fight harder. They keep our country safe.

Rangers lead their team.
They are ready for a raid.

Glossary

combat Fighting in a war.

compound A group of buildings that is sometimes surrounded by walls or a fence.

grenade A small bomb or explosive that can be thrown by hand or with a launcher.

parachute To jump from a plane with a parachute; also a large piece of strong and lightweight fabric with ropes that helps make a safe landing.

raid A sudden attack.

volunteer To offer to give a service.

weapon An object used in a fight to attack or defend.

Read More

Alvarez, Carlos. *Army Rangers.* Torque: Armed Forces. Minneapolis: Bellwether Media, 2010.

Besel, Jennifer M. *The Army Rangers.* Elite Military Forces. Mankato, Minn.: Capstone Press, 2011.

Gordon, Nick. *Army Rangers.* Epic Books: U.S. Military. Minneapolis: Bellwether Media, 2013.

Websites

About the Army Rangers: Military.com
www.military.com/special-operations/army-rangers.html

A Day in the Life of an Army Ranger
sofrep.com/army-rangers/a-day-in-the-life/

United States Army Rangers – The United States Army
www.army.mil/ranger/

Every effort has been made to ensure that these websites are appropriate for children. However, because of the nature of the Internet, it is impossible to guarantee that these sites will remain active indefinitely or that their contents will not be altered.

Index

bases 20–21
combat 24
compounds 4
enemies 4, 7, 8, 16, 23, 24, 27, 28
grenades 8
home front 19, 20
missions 8, 11, 16, 19, 20, 24
night vision goggles 5
overseas 23
parachuting 23
raids 4, 24
Ranger School 11, 12, 16
rescue missions 27
supplies 19, 24, 25
training 11, 12, 15, 16, 19
weapons 11, 16, 19

About the Author

Linda Bozzo is the author of more than 45 books for the school and library market. She would like to thank all of the men and women in the military for their outstanding service to our country. Visit her website at www.lindabozzo.com.

$28.50
10-14

T 575737